Dedication

This book is dedicated to my children:
Kiran and Tejas.
For the laughter, the love, the journey.
You inspire me to be my best
everyday.
I love you.

~Mom

Acknowledgements

Writing a book is harder than I thought and this book would not have been possible without the following people:

Thank you very much to Terry Beckwith and Ruby Singleton for planting the idea and helping it grow. I am eternally grateful to both of you for your part in bringing this story to life.

A special thank you to Alex Rosenberg, who brought the vision and form of this story alive through his exemplary illustrations.

Finally, to my husband and partner, Chetan – for getting this book to the finish line, always cheering me on and being a part of this journey. I love you.

Tejas is a boy with a dog named Duchess.
They are best friends.
Tejas goes for walks with Duchess to Park Joy.
He loves to play in Park Joy.

Duchess loves walking to Park Joy with Tejas.
She runs around in the park.
Tejas throws a ball in the park and waits for
Duchess to bring the ball back to him.

Today they are going to Park Joy.
Tejas wears braces to help him walk.
The braces hurt his feet. The pain is okay
when he is at the park with Duchess.
Tejas plays with the other kids and says Hi to
everyone he sees.

Park Joy is a short walk from home.
Tejas walks slow because his legs are not strong.
Duchess walks slow so Tejas can keep up.
Tejas and Duchess walk together side-by-side.

On their way to the park, they meet a woman
named Pity and her small baby.
Tejas says Hi to Pity.
Pity asks Tejas how old he is.
He says "7" and Pity is startled.
Tejas tells Pity how much he loves music while
Pity looks at her baby.

Duchess wants to keep walking and pulls Tejas away.
Tejas waves Bye as he walks away.
Pity continues to speak, not realizing Tejas and
Duchess have left.

Tejas and Duchess take more steps towards the park.
Tejas is tired and decides to sit on a ledge in front of a house.
Duchess sits next to him.

A man named Kind stops and smiles at Tejas and Duchess.
Tejas says Hi and points to Park Joy.
He tells Kind about the park and slide.
Kind listens carefully.

Tejas shows Kind and Duchess his shadow because shadows are cool!

Kind realizes he must go and says Bye.

As Tejas waves Bye to Kind, Kind looks back and says goodbye.

Duchess tugs at Tejas to keep walking toward the park.

APATHY
4
7

Tejas and Duchess are almost at the park but Tejas' feet hurt.
They come across a group of older boys playing soccer.
Tejas reads Apathy on the back of one of the boys' shirts.

APATHY
4

Tejas walks towards them to join in.

As the ball nears, Tejas slowly bends down to pick up the ball to throw to Duchess.

Apathy is very fast and kicks the ball away.

Tejas loses his balance and as he falls forward, looks up to make sure Duchess is near.

Duchess barks as Tejas says, 'I'm okay.'
Duchess watches Tejas to make sure he does not fall again.
Tejas' balance is shaky but he stands up straight.
Now that Tejas is ready, Duchess pulls him toward the entrance of the park.

PARK

Tejas and Duchess are at the entrance of the park.
As Tejas looks at the slide, he can feel pain in his feet.
He turns to Duchess for help.
She nudges him forward to say "You can do this, keep going."

Tejas and Duchess walk to the swing.
Tejas sits on the swing, balances himself into position and quickly holds onto the ropes.
As he swings, he yells, "My legs back, my legs out."
Tejas is smiling; his feet no longer hurt and a cool breeze falls on his face.
Duchess barks to let him know she wants to play ball with him.

HOME

Tejas and Duchess play for a long time together at the park.
The Sun is now setting and dusk is about to settle over the
park.
As Tejas and Duchess walk home, Tejas says "I love you
Duchess." Duchess barks to Tejas.
Tejas and Duchess' family is happy they are home in time for
dinner.

THE END